THE SNOWY DAY

TIPS FOR READING WITH PRESCHOOLERS

Here are some ways to get the most out of reading **The Snowy Day** *and other books with your preschooler:*

• Have your child look at the pictures and tell the story. Ask, "What is Peter making out of snow?"

• Ask questions about the story such as: what might have happened before the story started, what's going on now, and what may come next. Ask, "What do you think will happen to the snowball in Peter's pocket?"

• Use the story to start a conversation. Say, "Snow is cold and white. What are some other things that are cold? What are some other things that are white?"

• Point out words. Point to and spell "snow" each time you see it on the page. Pause to let your child recognize and "read" the word.

Here are some ways you can extend your preschooler's learning "on the go":

• Point out things from the books you've read as you travel around town. "Look, there is a snowman like Peter made in the story we read."

• Talk about books during your daily routines. During your child's bath time, ask "What was Peter thinking about when he took a bath?"

THE SNOWY DAY

Also by Ezra Jack Keats

Whistle for Willie

Clementina's Cactus

EZRA JACK KEATS

THE
SNOWY
DAY

New York · The Viking Press

VIKING
A Division of Penguin Books USA Inc.
375 Hudson Street   New York, New York 10014
Penguin Books Ltd, 27 Wrights Lane, London W8 5TZ England
Penguin Books Australia Ltd, Ringwood, Victoria, Australia
Penguin Books Canada Ltd, 10 Alcorn Avenue, Toronto, Ontario, Canada M4V 3B2
Penguin Books (N.Z.) Ltd, 182-190 Wairau Road, Auckland 10, New Zealand

Penguin Books Ltd, Registered Offices: Harmondsworth, Middlesex, England

First published in 1962 by Viking Penguin Inc.
Published simultaneously in Canada
Copyright © Ezra Jack Keats, 1962
All rights reserved
Library of Congress catalog number: 62-15441
Special Markets ISBN 978-0-670-06259-1
Not for Resale
Manufactured in China
Set in Bembo
7 9 10 8 6

This Imagination Library edition is published by Penguin Group (USA), a Pearson
company, exclusively for Dolly Parton's Imagination Library, a not-for-profit
program designed to inspire a love of reading and learning, sponsored in part by The Dolly-
wood Foundation. Penguin's trade editions of this work are available wherever books are sold.

To Tick, John, and Rosalie

One winter morning Peter woke up
and looked out the window. Snow
had fallen during the night. It cov-
ered everything as far as he could see.

After breakfast he put on his snowsuit and ran outside. The snow was piled up very high along the street to make a path for walking.

Crunch, crunch, crunch, his feet sank into the snow.
He walked with his toes pointing out, like this:

He walked with his toes
pointing in, like that:

Then he dragged his feet s-l-o-w-l-y
to make tracks.

And he found something sticking out
of the snow that made a new track.

It was a stick

— a stick that was just right for smacking a snow-covered tree.

Down fell the snow —
plop!
— on top of Peter's head.

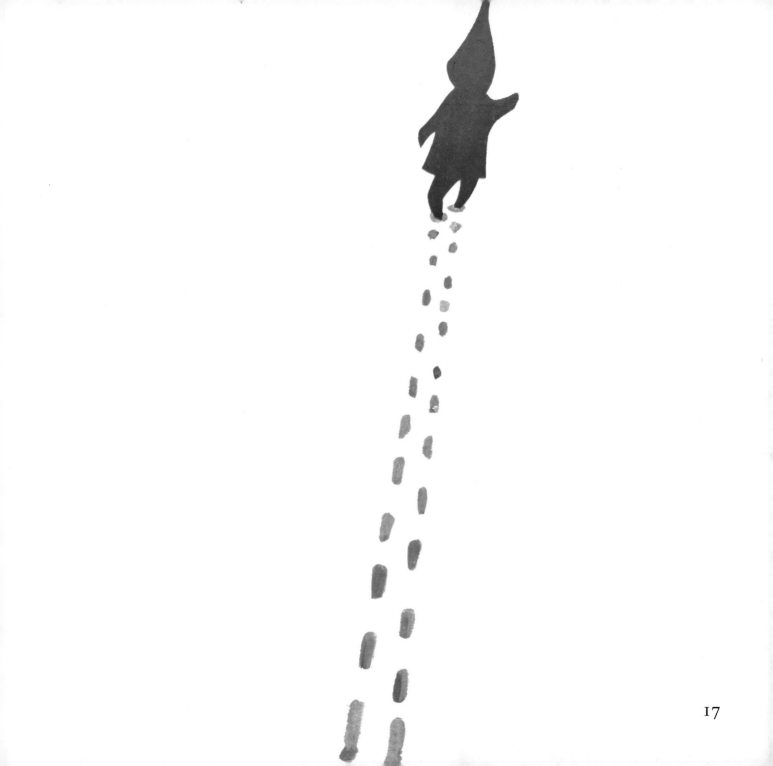

17

18

He thought it would be fun to join the big boys in their snowball fight, but he knew he wasn't old enough — not yet.

So he made a smiling snowman,

and he made angels.

He pretended
he was a mountain-climber.
He climbed up
a great big tall
heaping mountain of snow —

and slid all the way down.

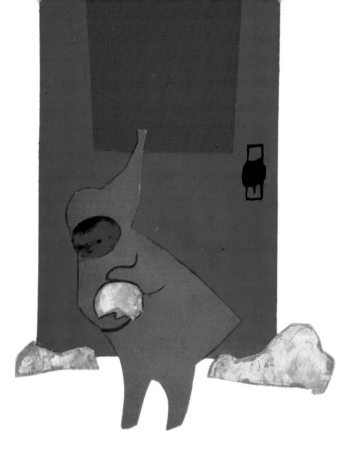

He picked up a handful of snow — and another,
and still another. He packed it round and firm and
put the snowball in his pocket for tomorrow. Then
he went into his warm house.

He told his mother all about his adventures
while she took off his wet socks.

And he thought and thought
and thought about them.

Before he got into bed he looked in his pocket.

His pocket was empty. The snowball wasn't there.

He felt very sad.

While he slept, he dreamed that the sun
had melted all the snow away.

But when he woke up his dream was gone.

The snow was still everywhere.

New snow was falling!

After breakfast he called to his
friend from across the hall, and
they went out together into the
deep, deep snow.